Persis Beach Bennett

Persis Beach Bennett lived in the house her father built in Lancaster, N.H. Her four children were born in that house. In 1915, about the time her last child was born, she began to have trouble seeing. By 1925, she was almost completely blind. Her blindness, however, never stopped her from enjoying life. She loved music and spent much of her time playing the piano and composing songs - recorded on 78 rpm records in 1949. Most of her music was Christian-based and ballads, but she delighted her grandchildren by writing five songs for and about them. Those songs are part of this book — *I Can't See, But...I Can Imagine.*

Beulah Bennett Sayles

Beulah Bennett Sayles, daughter of Persis, was a self-taught, but accomplished, pianist. Not only was she the pianist on the original recordings, but she spent many years after her mother's death writing the music down. When the recordings deteriorated over time, it was the written music that saved the day.

Dedicated to Bobby, Shayne, Brandon and Trevor - her great-great grandchildren

BOOK:

AUTHOR	Patricia Bennett Wilson, Redmond, OR
SONG WRITER	Persis Beach Bennett (diseased 1954), Lancaster, NH
ILLUSTRATOR	Sharon Bean, Madras, OR
DESIGNER	UDG DesignWorks, Sisters, OR
PUBLISHER	Global Publishing Services, Jason Millikan, Bend OR

© 2003 Patricia Bennett Wilson

AUDIO CD:

STORY TELLER	Elise Michaels, Bend, OR
GRAMMIE	Lois Webb, Sunriver, OR
THE FROG SONG	Blane Cameron, Redmond, OR Gracie Gillem, Bend, OR
ROCK-A-BYE TOWN	Dee Werner, Madras, OR
PATTY'S PUPPY PEPPER	Lori Starr, Redmond, OR
SWINGING FROM A STAR	Dee Werner, Madras, OR
MARY LOU	Gracie Gillem, Bend, OR
PIANIST	Steven J. Samples, Bend, OR
SOUND STUDIO	Soundsmith Recording Studio, Clay Smith, Bend, OR

I Can't See, But...
I Can Imagine

by Patricia Bennett Wilson

Illustrated by Sharon Bean

Richardson St.

A long time ago Patty's grandmother lived in a big house on a hill on

Richardson Street. When Patty was a little girl, visiting her grandmother was

one of her most favorite things to do. Grammie always made Patty feel special.

She did all the wonderful things grandmothers do. She made her

granddaughter laugh, gave her hugs, and told her stories.

Patty loved to help Grammie bake cookies

She liked to stir the cookie dough, but first she watched

her grandmother put all the ingredients in the bowl.

Before each ingredient went in the bowl, Grammie measured it by

feeling it in her hands. You see, Patty's grandmother was blind.

One day, Grammie asked Patty, "Will you walk downstreet with me?"

Patty felt so grown up! She knew her grandmother trusted her to tell her

where to step. Grammie loved walking downstreet, because she

always saw lots of friends.

Once Patty asked, "Grammie, what is it like not to be able to see?"

Grammie said, "Oh, Patty, it isn't so bad. I wasn't always blind.

I can still do lots of things. I cook. I play the piano. I have lots of friends.

I love to be with all my family, especially my five grandchildren:

you, Patty, and Doreen, Carl, Janie, and Rodney."

She said, "I can't see…BUT…I CAN IMAGINE. Imagining how things look is very exciting." Patty loved listening to her grandmother tell how she imagined things.

A very special thing Grammie did was write music.
She said, "I IMAGINE how things look around me, and then I write a song about them."
Often, Patty would sit next to her grandmother on the piano bench watching her play the piano and listening to her sing her songs.
Many times Grammie's songs would make Patty laugh.

One day Grammie told Patty about the time she
and Patty's cousin Doreen were at the lake.
She said, "There was a little inlet of water close to
the shore. A great big bullfrog was sitting on a log. Across the
inlet, there was a little frog — a tad —
sitting in the water on a lily pad. They seemed
to be talking back and forth.
'CROAK! CROAK! Peep! Peep!
CROAK! CROAK! Peep! Peep!'
They talked for the longest time!"
"Pretty soon a motorboat came by and made a wave
that swept the big frog off his log. Doreen noticed that the little
tad stayed up on his lily pad — as pretty as you please!
Doreen laughed and I laughed so hard!
I couldn't see the frogs, but I could IMAGINE what they looked like,
and what they were saying ......so I wrote a song."

THE FROG SONG

"Croak! Croak!" said the big bullfrog, sittin' on a mossy log.

"Peep! Peep!" said the little tad, restin' on a lily pad.

"Croak! Croak, I'm fair to see! Don't you wish you were big like me?"

"Peep! Peep! Your vanity! Once you were little, just like me!"

"Croak! Croak! Who told you so? Come now, I want to know."

"Little bird in the big pine tree Peep! Peep! told it to me."

"Croak! Croak! What can you do? Can't even catch a fly or two!"

"Yes I could, if I should try, but who wants a sour fly?"

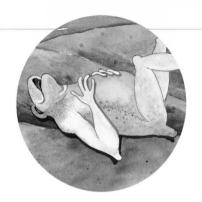

"Croak! Croak!" said the big bullfrog. "You can't even sit on a log!"

"Peep! Peep!" said the little tad. "You can't rest on a lily pad!"

Just then a big wave came rollin' along and swept Mr. Frog right off'a that log.

"Peep! Peep!" and he laughed with glee, "How's about that, you big froggy!"

"Croak! Croak!" said the big bullfrog. "I's-a tired of sittin' on that log."

"Peep! Peep! You can't fool me! That's a big joke, you big froggy!"

With a " Croak! Croak!" and a sheepish grin, "I guess that I can't always win."

"We all make mistakes, so don't feel bad. Peep Peep!" said the little tad.

"Peep Peep!" said the little tad.

"Croak! Croak!" "Peep! Peep!"

One time Grammie told Patty, "I spend lots of time rocking my grandchildren. When your cousin Janie was a baby, I loved to rock her. The rocking chair creaked every time it went back and forth – back and forth. I wanted to sing Janie a lullaby so that she would sleep. As Janie slept, I could IMAGINE that the rocking chair was a chariot and we were going to Rock-a-Bye town….so I wrote a song."

ROCK-A-BYE TOWN

Little Janie and Grammie,

On a rocking spree.

The rocking chair is a chariot,

With its ponies three.

Rocking, rocking, to and fro.

See the ponies go!

Surely by sundown,

They'll come to

ROCK-A-BYE TOWN.

Little Janie is tired

From her day at play.

From morning to sundown,

That's a very long day.

Now she's come to Grammie,

And her ponies three.

At sundown, in ROCK-A-BYE TOWN,

The sandman they do see.

ROCK-A-BYE TOWN
this-a-way
POPULATION
a goodly number
POP. SLUMBERLAND
more than that
over

Tired little eyelids,

Falling on the cheek.

The rocking chair rocks slower,

Hear the chariot creak.

The sandman is watching,

As the sun goes down.

The ponies are returning

Home from ROCK-A-BYE TOWN.

ROCK-A-BYE TOWN MMMMMMMMMM……

Patty was delighted when her grandmother wrote a song about
her and her dog Pepper. One day, she taught Patty how to play it with
one finger on the piano.

Grammie said, "One summer we were on a beach near our cottage
on the lake. You and your cousin Carl were playing with Pepper.
I couldn't see the three of you, but I could hear you…and I could IMAGINE
everything that was happening….so I wrote a song."

PATTY'S PUPPY PEPPER

Patty has a puppy, Pepper is her name.

Pepper doesn't have a pedigree of fame.

For she is a mongrel, that's not hard to see.

But Patty's little Pepper is cute as she can be.

Her nose is long and pointed. On the end it's black.

And she has a dark streak running down her back.

Her legs are long and slender, ears flop up and down.

And when she tries to catch her long tail, she goes round and round.

Vacation in the summer - up to the lake,

Patty, Carl and Pepper, much fun did make.

Playing in the sand and building castles fine,

Patty, Carl and Pepper, they had a jolly time.

Jumping in the water with a big

POW WOW,

Pepper on the shore answering

"BOW WOW!"

They threw her in the water.

She scrambled to the shore,

Shook herself and ran around and

BOW WOW WOW'd some more.

If you want a friend that's always good and true,

One that will be always waiting for you,

Get a little puppy; a mongrel one will do.

And like Patty's Pepper, she'll be a pal to you!

That's right!

Grammie told Patty about another adventure she imagined
in her rocking chair. "When I was rocking your cousin Rodney,
I began to IMAGINE that my rocking chair was a swing.
My! How high that swing could go! It seemed we were so high
that Rodney and I were swinging from a star…so I wrote a song."

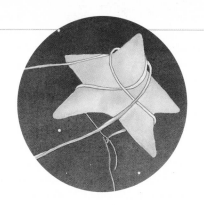

SWINGING FROM A STAR

Come my little honey child - little curly head.

Come, let's rock a little while 'fore you go to bed.

As the lullabies I sing, we're way up high on a swing,

Swinging, swinging from a star - swinging near and far.

All the little bluebirds fly – home to rest.

As we go a-swinging by, we'll see them in their nest.

Close those big shiny eyes while I sing the lullaby.

Swinging, swinging to and fro, to Slumberland we go.

Close those big shiny eyes while I sing the lullaby.

Swinging, swinging to and fro, to Slumberland we go.

MMMMMMMMmmmmmmmmmmmmm

Grammie said, "I live in the same house with two of my grandchildren,

Janie and Carl. When Janie was three, she had a doll she loved.

Her name was Mary Lou. I couldn't see the doll, but I could feel her

with my hands. I could IMAGINE what she looked like…so I wrote a song."

MARY LOU

I have a little dolly. I call her Mary Lou.

I had that little dolly long 'fore I was two.

My dolly Mary Lou is just a stockin' doll,

Buttons for her eyes and no teeth a'tall .

And her hair is phony – stands right on end.

I guess she needs a Toni®, to make it bend.

Mary Lou, Mary Lou - I only think of you!

I wouldn't have, my Mary Lou, a prettier doll than you!

When I go to bed at night -

where the shadows creep,

Mary Lou I cuddle tight.

Soon we're fast asleep.

When the sun awakens me to a morning new,

Then I open wide my eyes. There's my Mary Lou.

Mary Lou, Mary Lou - I only think of you!

I wouldn't have, my Mary Lou, a prettier doll than you!

Mary Lou, Mary Lou - I only think of you!

I wouldn't have, my Mary Lou, a prettier doll than you!

'Cause you are my little doll, I love you.

MARY LOU

Patty and her four cousins — Carl, Doreen, Janie, Rodney —

are grown up and have children and grandchildren of their own.

They love to teach them the songs their grandmother wrote.

Patty often tells the children about their great-grandmother.

She says, "Grammie is in Heaven now.

I don't know what heaven looks like,

BUT...I CAN IMAGINE."